To Nicolas and Greyson, sweetest of dreams.
— R H

To Mark, for all your patience and support,
and to the landscapes of Garden Hill.
— Q L

Text copyright © 2015 by Robert Heidbreder
Illustrations copyright © 2015 by Qin Leng
Published in Canada and the USA in 2015 by Groundwood Books

Groundwood Books / House of Anansi Press
110 Spadina Avenue, Suite 801, Toronto, Ontario M5V 2K4
or c/o Publishers Group West
1700 Fourth Street, Berkeley, CA 94710

We acknowledge for their financial support of our publishing program the
Canada Council for the Arts, the Government of Canada through
the Canada Book Fund (CBF) and the Ontario Arts Council.

Canada Council **Conseil des Arts**
for the Arts **du Canada**

ONTARIO ARTS COUNCIL
CONSEIL DES ARTS DE L'ONTARIO
an Ontario government agency
un organisme du gouvernement de l'Ontario

Library and Archives Canada Cataloguing in Publication
Heidbreder, Robert, author
Song for a summer night : a lullaby / written by Robert
Heidbreder ; illustrated by Qin Leng.
Issued in print and electronic formats.
ISBN 978-1-55498-493-0 (bound).—ISBN 978-1-55498-494-7 (pdf)
I. Leng, Qin, illustrator II. Title.
PS8565.E42S66 2015   jC811'.54   C2014-905902-7
C2014-905903-5

The illustrations were done with ink and brush and painted digitally.
Design by Michael Solomon
Printed and bound in Malaysia

FSC
www.fsc.org
MIX
Paper from
responsible sources
FSC® C012700

Song for a Summer Night

A Lullaby

Robert Heidbreder

Pictures by
Qin Leng

Groundwood Books House of Anansi Press Toronto Berkeley

Day's left the stage.
Night's in the wings.
The summer air sings
what a summer night brings.

Draw back the curtains.
     The still park's below.
     The children at windows
          all wait for night's show.

Tall tree branches arch
    to frame the stage well.
Thick, whispering leaves
    tell of night's spell.

    shh-shh

Fireflies' glint-glints
    sparkle the scene,
    earth-stars glimmering
        a shimmering green.
            shh-shh
            glint-glint

Now bellflowers ring,
    pring-pring with a chime,
    and in waltz raccoons
    in tra-la-la time.

    shh-shh
    glint-glint
    pring-pring
    tra-la-la

Snapdragons snap-snap
  to keep up the beat,
  while children at windows
  tip-tap their feet.

shh-shh
glint-glint
pring-pring
tra-la-la
snap-snap
tip-tap

Night owl hoo-hoos
Weave a musical strain
to the click-click of crickets'
rhythmic refrain.

shh-shh
glint-glint
pring-pring
tra-la-la
snap-snap
tip-tap
hoo-hoo
click-click

Black cats purr-purr,
   tails held high.
   They pounce on the moonbeams
   that fall from the sky.

shh-shh   hoo-hoo
glint-glint   click-click
pring-pring   purr-purr
   tra-la-la
   snap-snap
   tip-tap

Sniffing out food,
shy skunks scratch-scratch,
finding a feast
in a grassy patch.

shh-shh   tip-tap
glint-glint   hoo-hoo
pring-pring   click-click
tra-la-la   purr-purr
snap-snap   scratch-scratch

In bounce some dogs
with happy leap-bounds.
Their drumming pound-pounds
round out the park sounds.

shh-shh
glint-glint
pring-pring
tra-la-la
snap-snap
tip-tap
hoo-hoo
click-click
purr-purr
scratch-scratch
pound-pound

The children are spellbound,
    attuned to the park.
Its music brightens,
    lightens the dark.

While night air keeps singing
its soft lullaby,
the tired-out moon
seeks its bed in the sky.

Then animals leave,
    on feet or on wings,
    but the summer night song
    lingers on as it sings :

shh - shh
glint - glint
    pring - pring
        tra - la - la
    snap - snap
    tip - tap
hoo - hoo
click - click
purr - purr
scratch - scratch
    pound - pound

Now night stage stands empty,
darkened and still.
Children pull curtains
on each window sill.

They slip into beds,
eyes shut sleep-tight.
They know singing dreams
will ring round them all night.

shh-shh
glint-glint
pring-pring
tra-la-la
snap-snap
tip-tap
hoo-hoo
click-click
purr-purr
scratch-scratch
pound-pound

Soon morning turns bright,
with sun hiding moon,
and children greet day,
humming night's tune.

All through day's play,
soft strains come and go,
as children await
a new nighttime show.